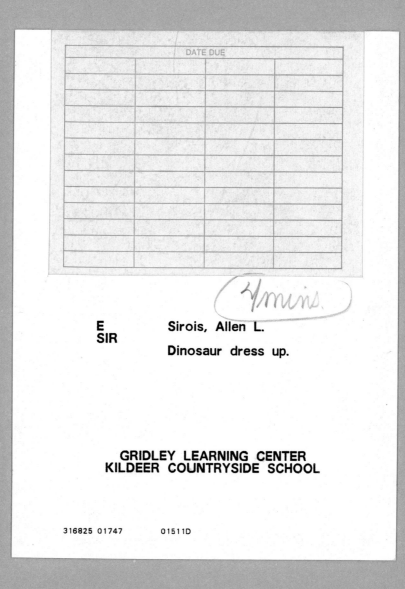

4mins.

E
SIR

Sirois, Allen L.

Dinosaur dress up.

**GRIDLEY LEARNING CENTER
KILDEER COUNTRYSIDE SCHOOL**

DINOSAUR DRESS UP

by
Allen L. Sirois

pictures by
Janet Street

Tambourine Books   New York

Inquiries should be addressed to Tambourine Books,
a division of William Morrow & Company, Inc.,
1350 Avenue of the Americas,
New York, New York 10019.
Printed in Italy

The full-color illustrations were painted in
watercolor on cold-press paper.

Library of Congress Cataloging in Publication Data
Sirois, Allen L. Dinosaur dress up/by Allen L. Sirois;
pictures by Janet Street.—1st ed.   p.   cm.
Summary: Professor Saurus describes the clothing
habits of dinosaurs and how their obsession with fashion
led to their extinction.
ISBN 0-688-10459-2 (trade)—ISBN 0-688-10460-6 (lib.)
[1. Dinosaurs—Fiction.   2. Clothing and dress—Fiction.]
I. Street, Janet, ill.   II. Title.
PZ7.S6218Di 1992 [E]—dc20 91-10583 CIP AC

1 3 5 7 9 10 8 6 4 2
First edition

To my parents
A.L.S.

To Casey and Rachel
J.S.

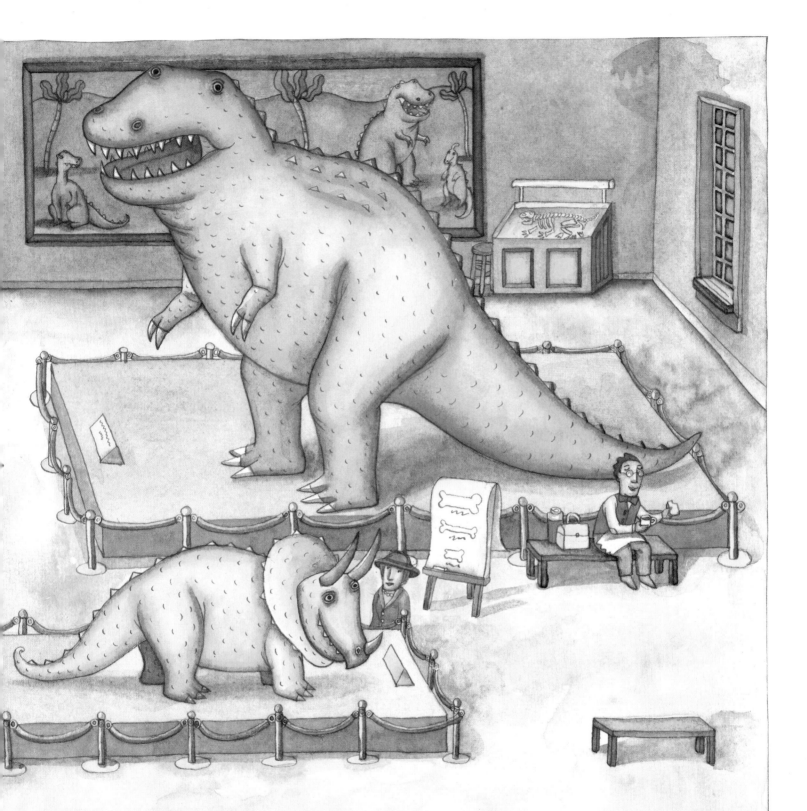

My friend Professor Saurus is the curator of the Hall of Dinosaurs. I can always find him at noon having lunch behind the tyrannosaurus rex.

He knows more secrets
about dinosaurs than anyone
in the world.

He even claims to know why
they died off, leaving behind
nothing more than fossils.

The other day Professor Saurus told me a secret he figured out only after many years of studying those old bones.

Dinosaurs wore clothing!

Dinosaurs loved clothes. They stuffed their closets full
of trousers and dresses, ties and belts, blouses and shirts
and hats.

When they went to the beach they wore bikinis and water wings. And for exercising they had sweat suits, headbands, and crest warmers.

They had clothes for cooking,
ballet dancing, camping and hiking,
playing baseball, programming computers,
and of course for going on vacation.

They had safety clothes for riding bicycles—
and even costumes for their little dinosaur dolls!

Professor Saurus insisted all
dinosaurs delighted in clothes—
even though the styles young
dinosaurs admired most were ones
their parents hated.

In fact, he said, most dinosaurs
had so many outfits that at times
they couldn't decide what to wear.

What dinosaurs enjoyed best of all was dressing up for a night on the town.

They'd spend hours choosing a wardrobe, putting on makeup, shaving, washing their scales, polishing their teeth, and curling their tails.

How splendid they must have looked parading in the prehistoric twilight! Gentlemen with their top hats, silk ties, and jeweled stickpins, and ladies in fine gowns,

necklaces, and diamond tiaras. Of course they loved
to rock and roll! They danced till the earth shook,
all night long.

At dawn they'd yawn,
then creep home and fall
into bed. The next night
they'd be ready to do it all
over again.

The dinosaurs lived happily this way for millions and millions of years. Finally some dinosaurs— the ones who didn't have so much clothing—got jealous of the ones who had lots to wear. They started to squabble.

They disagreed about who had the finest fashions.
They argued over who had the biggest wardrobe.

They fought about who had the most original styles.

They disagreed and argued and fought and got so mad that they tore each other's clothing to shreds!

But the fighting didn't stop there. They couldn't agree on what kind of new clothes to make, or even who should make them. Dino designers and models fought over fabrics and colors and ruffles and buttons.

While the dinosaurs were standing around arguing in their underwear they couldn't keep from catching cold. Their colds developed into pneumonia, and they started to die.

Before long, hardly any dinosaurs were left.

"The only ones who saved themselves were the ones with wings," Professor Saurus said, leading me into

another exhibition hall. "When all the fighting started,
they flew far away to safety.

"Over many years, they changed. They became smaller and their scales grew out into feathers. Nowadays they don't look much like dinosaurs, so most people don't recognize them.

"But you can tell that that's
what they used to be, because
large or small, they have always
loved to wear beautiful patterns
and bright colors!"